Apocolocyntosis

Lucius Seneca

Contents

APOCOLOCYNTOSIS

BY

Lucius Seneca

SENECA
APOCOLOCYNTOSIS

INTRODUCTION

This piece is ascribed to Seneca by ancient tradition; it is impossible to prove that it is his, and impossible to prove that it is not. The matter will probably continue to be decided by every one according to his view of Seneca's character and abilities: in the matters of style and of sentiment much may be said on both sides. Dion Cassius (lx, 35) says that Seneca composed an [Greek: apokolokuntosis] or Pumpkinification of Claudius after his death, the title being a parody of the usual [Greek: apotheosis]; but this title is not given in the MSS. of the Ludus de Morte Claudii, nor is there anything in the piece which suits the title very well.

As a literary form, the piece belongs to the class called **Satura Menippea**, a satiric medley in prose and verse.

This text is that of Buecheler, with a few trifling changes, which are indicated in the notes. We have been courteously allowed by Messrs Weidmann to use this text. I have to acknowledge the help of Mr Ball's notes, from which I have taken a few references; but my translation was made many years ago.

W.H.D. ROUSE.

SENECA

APOCOLOCYNTOSIS,

OR LUDUS DE MORTE CLAUDII:
THE PUMPKINIFICATION OF CLAUDIUS.

I wish to place on record the proceedings in heaven October 13 last, of the new year which begins this auspicious age. It shall be done without malice or favour. This is the truth. Ask if you like how I know it? To begin with, I am not bound to please you with my answer. Who will compel me? I know the same day made me free, which was the last day for him who made the proverb true—One must be born either a Pharaoh or a fool. If I choose to answer, I will say whatever trips off my tongue. Who has ever made the historian produce witness to swear for him? But if an authority must be produced, ask of the man who saw Drusilla translated to heaven: the same man will aver he saw Claudius on the road, dot and carry one.[1] Will he nill he, all that happens in heaven he needs must see. He is the custodian of the Appian Way; by that route, you know, both Tiberius and Augustus went up to the gods. Question him, he will tell you the tale when you are alone; before company he is dumb. You see he swore in the Senate that he beheld Drusilla mounting heavenwards, and all he got for his good news was that everybody gave him the lie: since when he solemnly swears he will never bear witness again to what he has seen, not even if he had seen a man murdered in open market. What he told me I report plain and clear, as I hope for his health and happiness.

---

1 Virg. Aen. ii, 724

Now had the sun with shorter course drawn in his risen light,
And by equivalent degrees grew the dark hours of night:
Victorious Cynthia now held sway over a wider space,
Grim winter drove rich autumn out, and now usurped his place;
And now the fiat had gone forth that Bacchus must grow old,
The few last clusters of the vine were gathered ere the cold:

I shall make myself better understood, if I say the month was October, the day was the thirteenth. What hour it was I cannot certainly tell; philosophers will agree more often than clocks; but it was between midday and one after noon. "Clumsy creature!" you say. "The poets are not content to describe sunrise and sunset, and now they even disturb the midday siesta. Will you thus neglect so good an hour?"

Now the sun's chariot had gone by the middle of his way;
Half wearily he shook the reins, nearer to night than day,
And led the light along the slope that down before him lay.

Claudius began to breathe his last, and could not make an end of the matter. Then Mercury, who had always been much pleased with his wit, drew aside one of the three Fates, and said: "Cruel beldame, why do you let the poor wretch be tormented? After all this torture cannot he have a rest? Four and sixty years it is now since he began to pant for breath. What grudge is this you bear against him and the whole empire? Do let the astrologers tell the truth for once; since he became emperor, they have never let a year pass, never a month, without laying him out for his burial. Yet it is no wonder if they are wrong, and no one knows his hour. Nobody ever believed he was really quite born.[2] Do what has to be done: Kill him, and let a better man rule in empty court."[3]

Clotho replied: "Upon my word, I did wish to give him another hour or two, until he should make Roman citizens of the half dozen who are still outsiders. (He made up his mind, you know, to see the whole world in the toga, Greeks, Gauls,

---

2 A proverb for a nobody, as Petron, **58 qui te natum non putat.**
3 Virg. Georg iv. 90

Spaniards, Britons, and all.) But since it is your pleasure to leave a few foreigners for seed, and since you command me, so be it." She opened her box and out came three spindles. One was for Augurinus, one for Baba, one for Claudius.[4] "These three," she says, "I will cause to die within one year and at no great distance apart, and I will not dismiss him unattended. Think of all the thousands of men he was wont to see following after him, thousands going before, thousands all crowding about him, and it would never do to leave him alone on a sudden. These boon companions will satisfy him for the nonce."

> This said, she twists the thread around his ugly spindle once,
> Snaps off the last bit of the life of that Imperial dunce.
> But Lachesis, her hair adorned, her tresses neatly bound,
> Pierian laurel on her locks, her brows with garlands crowned,
> Plucks me from out the snowy wool new threads as white as snow,
> Which handled with a happy touch change colour as they go,
> Not common wool, but golden wire; the Sisters wondering gaze,
> As age by age the pretty thread runs down the golden days.
> World without end they spin away, the happy fleeces pull;
> What joy they take to fill their hands with that delightful wool!
> Indeed, the task performs itself: no toil the spinners know:
> Down drops the soft and silken thread as round the spindles go;
> Fewer than these are Tithon's years, not Nestor's life so long.
> Phoebus is present: glad he is to sing a merry song;
> Now helps the work, now full of hope upon the harp doth play;
> The Sisters listen to the song that charms their toil away.
> They praise their brother's melodies, and still the spindles run,
> Till more than man's allotted span the busy hands have spun.
> Then Phoebus says, "O sister Fates! I pray take none away,
> But suffer this one life to be longer than mortal day.
> Like me in face and lovely grace, like me in voice and song,
> He'll bid the laws at length speak out that have been dumb so long,
> Will give unto the weary world years prosperous and bright.

---

4 "Augurinus" unknown. Baba: see Sep. Ep. 159, a fool.

Like as the daystar from on high scatters the stars of night,
As, when the stars return again, clear Hesper brings his light,
Or as the ruddy dawn drives out the dark, and brings the day,
As the bright sun looks on the world, and speeds along its way
His rising car from morning's gates: so Caesar doth arise,
So Nero shows his face to Rome before the people's eyes,
His bright and shining countenance illumines all the air,
While down upon his graceful neck fall rippling waves of hair."
Thus Apollo. But Lachesis, quite as ready to cast a
favourable eye on a handsome man, spins away by the
handful, and bestows years and years upon Nero out
of her own pocket. As for Claudius, they tell everybody
to speed him on his way
With cries of joy and solemn litany.

At once he bubbled up the ghost, and there was an end to that shadow of a life. He was listening to a troupe of comedians when he died, so you see I have reason to fear those gentry. The last words he was heard to speak in this world were these. When he had made a great noise with that end of him which talked easiest, he cried out, "Oh dear, oh dear! I think I have made a mess of myself." Whether he did or no, I cannot say, but certain it is he always did make a mess of everything.

What happened next on earth it is mere waste of time to tell, for you know it all well enough, and there is no fear of your ever forgetting the impression which that public rejoicing made on your memory. No one forgets his own happiness. What happened in heaven you shall hear: for proof please apply to my informant. Word comes to Jupiter that a stranger had arrived, a man well set up, pretty grey; he seemed to be threatening something, for he wagged his head ceaselessly; he dragged the right foot. They asked him what nation he was of; he answered something in a confused mumbling voice: his language they did not understand. He was no Greek and no Roman, nor of any known race. On this Jupiter bids Hercules go and find out what country he comes from; you see Hercules had travelled over the whole world, and might be expected to know all the nations in it. But Hercules, the first glimpse he got, was really much taken aback, although not all the monsters in the world could frighten him; when he saw this new kind of object, with its extraordinary gait, and the voice of no terrestrial beast, but such as you might hear in the leviathans of the deep, hoarse and inarticulate, he thought his thirteenth labour had come upon him. When he looked closer, the thing seemed to be a kind of man. Up he goes, then, and says what your Greek finds readiest to his tongue:

> "Who art thou, and what thy people? Who thy
> parents, where thy home?"[5]

Claudius was delighted to find literary men up there, and began to hope there might be some corner for his own historical works. So he caps him with another Homeric verse, explaining that he was Caesar:

> "Breezes wafted me from Ilion unto the Ciconian land."[6]

But the next verse was more true, and no less Homeric:

> "Thither come, I sacked a city, slew the people every one."

He would have taken in poor simple Hercules, but that Our Lady of Malaria was there, who left her temple and came alone with him: all the other gods he had left at Rome. Quoth she, "The fellow's tale is nothing but lies. I have lived with him all these years, and I tell you, he was born at Lyons. You behold a fellow-burgess of Marcus.[7] As I say, he was born at the sixteenth milestone from Vienne, a native Gaul. So of course he took Rome, as a good Gaul ought to do. I pledge you my word that in Lyons he was born, where Licinus[8] was king so many years. But you that have trudged over more roads than any muleteer that plies for hire, you must have come across the people of Lyons, and you must know that it is a far cry from Xanthus

---

5 Od. i, 17
6 Od. ix, 39
7 Reference unknown.
8 A Gallic slave, appointed by Augustus Procurator of Gallia Lugudunensis, when he made himself notorious by his extortions. See Dion Cass. liv, 21.

to the Rhone." At this point Claudius flared up, and expressed his wrath with as big a growl as he could manage. What he said nobody understood; as a matter of fact, he was ordering my lady of Fever to be taken away, and making that sign with his trembling hand (which was always steady enough for that, if for nothing else) by which he used to decapitate men. He had ordered her head to be chopped off. For all the notice the others took of him, they might have been his own freedmen.

Then Hercules said, "You just listen to me, and stop playing the fool. You have come to the place where the mice nibble iron.[9] Out with the truth, and look sharp, or I'll knock your quips and quiddities out of you." Then to make himself all the more awful, he strikes an attitude and proceeds in his most tragic vein:

> "Declare with speed what spot you claim by birth.
> Or with this club fall stricken to the earth!
> This club hath ofttimes slaughtered haughty kings!
> Why mumble unintelligible things?
> What land, what tribe produced that shaking head?
> Declare it! On my journey when I sped
> Far to the Kingdom of the triple King,
> And from the Main Hesperian did bring
> The goodly cattle to the Argive town,
> There I beheld a mountain looking down
> Upon two rivers: this the Sun espies
> Right opposite each day he doth arise.
> Hence, mighty Rhone, thy rapid torrents flow,
> And Arar, much in doubt which way to go,
> Ripples along the banks with shallow roll.
> Say, is this land the nurse that bred thy soul?"

These lines he delivered with much spirit and a bold front. All the same, he was not quite master of his wits, and had some fear of a blow from the fool. Claudius, seeing a mighty man before him, saw things looked serious and understood that

---

9 A proverb, found also in Herondas iii, 76: apparently fairy-land, the land of Nowhere.

here he had not quite the same pre-eminence as at Rome, where no one was his equal: the Gallic cock was worth most on his own dunghill. So this is what he was thought to say, as far as could be made out: "I did hope, Hercules, bravest of all the gods, that you would take my part with the rest, and if I should need a voucher, I meant to name you who know me so well. Do but call it to mind, how it was I used to sit in judgment before your temple whole days together during July and August. You know what miseries I endured there, in hearing the lawyers plead day and night. If you had fallen amongst these, you may think yourself very strong, but you would have found it worse than the sewers of Augeas: I drained out more filth than you did. But since I want..."

(Some pages have fallen out, in which Hercules must have been persuaded. The gods are now discussing what Hercules tells them).

"No wonder you have forced your way into the Senate House: no bars or bolts can hold against you. Only do say what species of god you want the fellow to be made. An Epicurean god he cannot be: for they have no troubles and cause none. A Stoic, then? How can he be globular, as Varro says, without a head or any other projection? There is in him something of the Stoic god, as I can see now: he has neither heart nor head. Upon my word, if he had asked this boon from Saturn, he would not have got it, though he kept up Saturn's feast all the year round, a truly Saturnalian prince. A likely thing he will get it from Jove, whom he condemned for incest as far as in him lay: for he killed his son-in-law Silanus, because Silanus had a sister, a most charming girl, called Venus by all the world, and he preferred to call her Juno. Why, says he, I want to know why, his own sister? Read your books, stupid: you may go half-way at Athens, the whole way at Alexandria. Because the mice lick meal at Rome, you say. Is this creature to mend our crooked ways? What goes on in his own closet he knows not;[10] and now he searches the regions of the sky, wants to be a god. Is it not enough that he has a temple in Britain, that savages worship him and pray to him as a god, so that they may find a fool[11] to have mercy upon them?"

At last it came into Jove's head, that while strangers were in the House it was not lawful to speak or debate. "My lords and gentlemen," said he, "I gave you leave

---

10   Perhaps alluding to a mock marriage of Silius and Messalina.

11   Again [GREEK: morou] for [GREEK: theou]

to ask questions, and you have made a regular farmyard[12] of the place. Be so good as to keep the rules of the House. What will this person think of us, whoever he is?" So Claudius was led out, and the first to be asked his opinion was Father Janus: he had been made consul elect for the afternoon of the next first of July,[13] being as shrewd a man as you could find on a summer's day: for he could see, as they say, before and behind.[14] He made an eloquent harangue, because his life was passed in the forum, but too fast for the notary to take down. That is why I give no full report of it, for I don't want to change the words he used. He said a great deal of the majesty of the gods, and how the honour ought not to be given away to every Tom, Dick, or Harry. "Once," said he, "it was a great thing to become a god; now you have made it a farce. Therefore, that you may not think I am speaking against one person instead of the general custom, I propose that from this day forward the godhead be given to none of those who eat the fruits of the earth, or whom mother earth doth nourish. After this bill has been read a third time, whosoever is made, said, or portrayed to be god, I vote he be delivered over to the bogies, and at the next public show be flogged with a birch amongst the new gladiators." The next to be asked was Diespiter, son of Vica Pota, he also being consul elect, and a moneylender; by this trade he made a living, used to sell rights of citizenship in a small way. Hercules trips me up to him daintily, and tweaks him by the ear. So he uttered his opinion in these words: "Inasmuch as the blessed Claudius is akin to the blessed Augustus, and also to the blessed Augusta, his grandmother, whom he ordered to be made a goddess, and whereas he far surpasses all mortal men in wisdom, and seeing that it is for the public good that there be some one able to join Romulus in devouring boiled turnips, I propose that from this day forth blessed Claudius be a god, to enjoy that honour with all its appurtenances in as full a degree as any other before him, and that a note to that effect be added to Ovid's Metamorphoses." The meeting was divided, and it looked as though Claudius was to win the day. For Hercules saw his iron was in the fire, trotted here and trotted there, saying, "Don't deny me; I make a point of the matter. I'll do as much for you again, when you like; you roll my log, and I'll roll

---

12 Proverb: meaning unknown.

13 Perhaps an allusion to the shortening of the consul's term, which was done to give more candidates a chance of the honour.

14 II, iii, 109; alluding here to Janus's double face.

yours: one hand washes another."

Then arose the blessed Augustus, when his turn came, and spoke with much eloquence.[15] "I call you to witness, my lords and gentlemen," said he, "that since the day I was made a god I have never uttered one word. I always mind my own business. But now I can keep on the mask no longer, nor conceal the sorrow which shame makes all the greater. Is it for this I have made peace by land and sea? For this have I calmed intestine wars? For this, laid a firm foundation of law for Rome, adorned it with buildings, and all that—my lords, words fail me; there are none can rise to the height of my indignation. I must borrow that saying of the eloquent Messala Corvinus, I am ashamed of my authority.[16] This man, my lords, who looks as though he could not hurt a fly, used to chop off heads as easily as a dog sits down. But why should I speak of all those men, and such men? There is no time to lament for public disasters, when one has so many private sorrows to think of. I leave that, therefore, and say only this; for even if my sister knows no Greek, I do: The knee is nearer than the shin.[17] This man you see, who for so many years has been masquerading under my name, has done me the favour of murdering two Julias, great-granddaughters of mine, one by cold steel and one by starvation; and one great grandson, L. Silanus—see, Jupiter, whether he had a case against him (at least it is your own if you will be fair.) Come tell me, blessed Claudius, why of all those you killed, both men and women, without a hearing, why you did not hear their side of the case first, before putting them to death? Where do we find that custom? It is not done in heaven. Look at Jupiter: all these years he has been king, and never did more than once to break Vulcan's leg,

'Whom seizing by the foot he cast from the threshold of the sky,'[18]

---

15 The speech seems to contain a parody of Augustus's style and sayings.
16 M. Valerius Messala Corvinus, appointed praefectus urbi, resigned within a week.
17 A proverb, like "Charity begins at home." The reading of the passage is uncertain; "sister" is only a conjecture, and it is hard to see why his sister should be mentioned.
18 Illiad i, 591

and once he fell in a rage with his wife and strung her up: did he do any killing? You killed Messalina, whose great-uncle I was no less than yours. 'I don't know,' did you say? Curse you! that is just it: not to know was worse than to kill. Caligula he went on persecuting even when he was dead. Caligula murdered his father-in-law, Claudius his son-in-law to boot. Caligula would not have Crassus' son called Great; Claudius gave him his name back, and took away his head. In one family he destroyed Crassus, Magnus, Scribonia, the Tristionias, Assario, noble though they were; Crassus indeed such a fool that he might have been emperor. Is this he you want now to make a god? Look at his body, born under the wrath of heaven! In fine, let him say the three words[19] quickly, and he may have me for a slave. God! who will worship this god, who will believe in him? While you make gods of such as he, no one will believe you to be gods. To be brief, my lords: if I have lived honourably among you, if I have never given plain speech to any, avenge my wrongs. This is my motion": then he read out his amendment, which he had committed to writing: "Inasmuch as the blessed Claudius murdered his father-in-law Appius Silanus, his two sons-in-law, Pompeius Magnus and L. Silanus, Crassus Frugi his daughter's father-in-law, as like him as two eggs in a basket, Scribonia his daughter's mother-in-law, his wife Messalina, and others too numerous to mention; I propose that strong measures be taken against him, that he be allowed no delay of process, that immediate sentence of banishment be passed on him, that he be deported from heaven within thirty days, and from Olympus within thirty hours."

This motion was passed without further debate. Not a moment was lost: Mercury screwed his neck and haled him to the lower regions, to that bourne "from which they say no traveller returns."[20] As they passed downwards along the Sacred Way, Mercury asked what was that great concourse of men? could it be Claudius' funeral? It was certainly a most gorgeous spectacle, got up regardless of expense, clear it was that a god was being borne to the grave: tootling of flutes, roaring of horns, an immense brass band of all sorts, such a din that even Claudius could hear it. Joy and rejoicing on every side, the Roman people walking about like free men. Agatho and a few pettifoggers were weeping for grief, and for once in a way they meant it. The Barristers were crawling out of their dark corners, pale and thin, with hardly a

---

19 Some formula such as ***ais esse meum***.
20 Catullus iii, 12.

breath in their bodies, as though just coming to life again. One of them when he saw
the pettifoggers putting their heads together, and lamenting their sad lot, up comes
he and says: "Did not I tell you the Saturnalia could not last for ever?"

When Claudius saw his own funeral train, he understood that he was dead. For
they were chanting his dirge in anapaests, with much mopping and mouthing:

"Pour forth your laments, your sorrow declare,
Let the sounds of grief rise high in the air:
For he that is dead had a wit most keen,
Was bravest of all that on earth have been.
Racehorses are nothing to his swift feet:
Rebellious Parthians he did defeat;
Swift after the Persians his light shafts go:
For he well knew how to fit arrow to bow,
Swiftly the striped barbarians fled:
With one little wound he shot them dead.
And the Britons beyond in their unknown seas,
Blue-shielded Brigantians too, all these
He chained by the neck as the Romans' slaves.
He spake, and the Ocean with trembling waves
Accepted the axe of the Roman law.
O weep for the man! This world never saw
One quicker a troublesome suit to decide,
When only one part of the case had been tried,
(He could do it indeed and not hear either side).
Who'll now sit in judgment the whole year round?
Now he that is judge of the shades underground
Once ruler of fivescore cities in Crete,
Must yield to his better and take a back seat.
Mourn, mourn, pettifoggers, ye venal crew,
And you, minor poets, woe, woe is to you!
And you above all, who get rich quick
By the rattle of dice and the three card trick."

Claudius was charmed to hear his own praises sung, and would have stayed longer to see the show. But the Talthybius[21] of the gods laid a hand on him, and led him across the Campus Martius, first wrapping his head up close that no one might know him, until betwixt Tiber and the Subway he went down to the lower regions.[22] His freedman Narcissus had gone down before him by a short cut, ready to welcome his master. Out he comes to meet him, smooth and shining (he had just left the bath), and says he: "What make the gods among mortals?" "Look alive," says Mercury, "go and tell them we are coming." Away he flew, quicker than tongue can tell. It is easy going by that road, all down hill. So although he had a touch of the gout, in a trice they were come to Dis's door. There lay Cerberus, or, as Horace puts it, the hundred-headed monster.[23] Claudius was a trifle perturbed (it was a little white bitch he used to keep for a pet) when he spied this black shag-haired hound, not at all the kind of thing you could wish to meet in the dark. In a loud voice he cried, "Claudius is coming!" All marched before him singing, "The lost is found, O let us rejoice together!"[24] Here were found C. Silius consul elect, Juncus the ex-praetor, Sextus Traulus, M. Helvius, Trogus, Cotta, Vettius Valens, Fabius, Roman Knights whom Narcissus had ordered for execution. In the midst of this chanting company was Mnester the mime, whom Claudius for honour's sake had made shorter by a head. The news was soon blown about that Claudius had come: to Messalina they throng: first his freedmen, Polybius, Myron, Harpocras, Amphaeus, Pheronactus, all sent before him by Claudius that he might not be unattended anywhere; next two prefects, Justus Catonius and Rufrius Pollio; then his friends, Saturninus, Lusius and Pedo Pompeius and Lupus and Celer Asinius, these of consular rank; last came his brother's daughter, his sister's daughter, sons-in-law, fathers and mothers-in-law, the whole family in fact. In a body they came to meet Claudius; and when Claudius saw them, he exclaimed, "Friends everywhere, on my word! How came you all here?" To this Pedo Pompeius answered, "What, cruel man? How came we here? Who but you sent us, you, the murderer of all the friends that ever you had?

21 Talthybius was a herald, and *nuntius* is obviously a gloss on this. He means Mercury.
22 By the Cloaca?
23 Odes ii, 13, 35
24 With a slight change, a cry used in the worship of Osiris.

To court with you! I'll show you where their lordships sit."

Pedo brings him before the judgement seat of Aeacus, who was holding court under the Lex Cornelia to try cases of murder and assassination. Pedo requests the judge to take the prisoner's name, and produces a summons with this charge: Senators killed, 35; Roman Knights, 221; others as the sands of the sea-shore for multitude.[25] Claudius finds no counsel. At length out steps P. Petronius, an old chum of his, a finished scholar in the Claudian tongue and claims a remand. Not granted. Pedo Pompeius prosecutes with loud outcry. The counsel for the defence tries to reply; but Aeacus, who is the soul of justice, will not have it. Aeacus hears the case against Claudius, refuses to hear the other side and passes sentence against him, quoting the line:

"As he did, so be he done by, this is justice undefiled."[26]

A great silence fell. Not a soul but was stupefied at this new way of managing matters; they had never known anything like it before. It was no new thing to Claudius, yet he thought it unfair. There was a long discussion as to the punishment he ought to endure. Some said that Sisyphus had done his job of porterage long enough; Tantalus would be dying of thirst, if he were not relieved; the drag must be put at last on wretched Ixion's wheel. But it was determined not to let off any of the old stagers, lest Claudius should dare to hope for any such relief. It was agreed that some new punishment must be devised: they must devise some new task, something senseless, to suggest some craving without result. Then Aeacus decreed he should rattle dice for ever in a box with no bottom. At once the poor wretch began his fruitless task of hunting for the dice, which for ever slipped from his fingers.

"For when he rattled with the box, and thought he now had got 'em.
The little cubes would vanish thro' the perforated bottom.
Then he would pick 'em up again, and once more set a-trying:
The dice but served him the same trick: away they went a-flying.
So still he tries, and still he fails; still searching long he lingers;

---

25 Il. ix, 385
26 A proverbial line.

And every time the tricksy things go slipping thro' his fingers.
Just so when Sisyphus at last once gets there with his boulder,
He finds the labour all in vain--it rolls down off his shoulder."

All on a sudden who should turn up but Caligula, and claims the man for a slave: brings witnesses, who said they had seen him being flogged, caned, fisticuffed by him. He is handed over to Caligula, and Caligula makes him a present to Aeacus. Aeacus delivers him to his freedman Menander, to be his law-clerk.

BIBLIOGRAPHY

Editio Princeps: Lucii Annaei Senecae in morte Claudii Caesaris Ludus nuper repertus: Rome, 1513.

Latest critical text: Franz Buecheler, Weidmann, 1904 (a reprint with a few changes of the text from a larger work, Divi Claudii [Greek: Apokolokuntosis] in the Symbola Philologorum Bonnensium, fasc. i, 1864).

Translations and helps: The Satire of Seneca on the Apotheosis of Claudius, by A.P. Ball (with introduction, notes, and translations): New York: Columbia University Press; London, Macmillan, 1902.

THE END

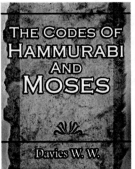

The Codes Of Hammurabi And Moses
W. W. Davies

QTY

The discovery of the Hammurabi Code is one of the greatest achievements of archaeology, and is of paramount interest, not only to the student of the Bible, but also to all those interested in ancient history...

Religion   ISBN: *1-59462-338-4*   **Pages:132**
MSRP $12.95

The Theory of Moral Sentiments
Adam Smith

QTY

This work from 1749. contains original theories of conscience amd moral judgment and it is the foundation for systemof morals.

Philosophy ISBN: *1-59462-777-0*   **Pages:536**
MSRP $19.95

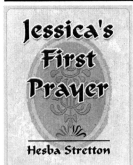

Jessica's First Prayer
Hesba Stretton

QTY

In a screened and secluded corner of one of the many railway-bridges which span the streets of London there could be seen a few years ago, from five o'clock every morning until half past eight, a tidily set-out coffee-stall, consisting of a trestle and board, upon which stood two large tin cans, with a small fire of charcoal burning under each so as to keep the coffee boiling during the early hours of the morning when the work-people were thronging into the city on their way to their daily toil...

Pages:84

Childrens   ISBN: *1-59462-373-2*   *MSRP $9.95*

My Life and Work
Henry Ford

QTY

Henry Ford revolutionized the world with his implementation of mass production for the Model T automobile. Gain valuable business insight into his life and work with his own auto-biography... "We have only started on our development of our country we have not as yet, with all our talk of wonderful progress, done more than scratch the surface. The progress has been wonderful enough but..."

Pages:300

Biographies/   ISBN: *1-59462-198-5*   *MSRP $21.95*

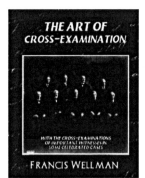

The Art of Cross-Examination
Francis Wellman

QTY

I presume it is the experience of every author, after his first book is published upon an important subject, to be almost overwhelmed with a wealth of ideas and illustrations which could readily have been included in his book, and which to his own mind, at least, seem to make a second edition inevitable. Such certainly was the case with me; and when the first edition had reached its sixth impression in five months, I rejoiced to learn that it seemed to my publishers that the book had met with a sufficiently favorable reception to justify a second and considerably enlarged edition. ...

Pages:412

Reference   **ISBN: *1-59462-647-2***   *MSRP $19.95*

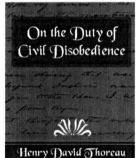

On the Duty of Civil Disobedience
Henry David Thoreau

QTY

Thoreau wrote his famous essay, On the Duty of Civil Disobedience, as a protest against an unjust but popular war and the immoral but popular institution of slave-owning. He did more than write—he declined to pay his taxes, and was hauled off to gaol in consequence. Who can say how much this refusal of his hastened the end of the war and of slavery ?

Law   **ISBN: *1-59462-747-9***   **Pages:48**

MSRP $7.45

Dream Psychology Psychoanalysis for Beginners
Sigmund Freud

QTY

Sigmund Freud, born Sigismund Schlomo Freud (May 6, 1856 - September 23, 1939), was a Jewish-Austrian neurologist and psychiatrist who co-founded the psychoanalytic school of psychology. Freud is best known for his theories of the unconscious mind, especially involving the mechanism of repression; his redefinition of sexual desire as mobile and directed towards a wide variety of objects; and his therapeutic techniques, especially his understanding of transference in the therapeutic relationship and the presumed value of dreams as sources of insight into unconscious desires.

Pages:196

Psychology   **ISBN: *1-59462-905-6***   *MSRP $15.45*

The Miracle of Right Thought
Orison Swett Marden

QTY

Believe with all of your heart that you will do what you were made to do. When the mind has once formed the habit of holding cheerful, happy, prosperous pictures, it will not be easy to form the opposite habit. It does not matter how improbable or how far away this realization may see, or how dark the prospects may be, if we visualize them as best we can, as vividly as possible, hold tenaciously to them and vigorously struggle to attain them, they will gradually become actualized, realized in the life. But a desire, a longing without endeavor, a yearning abandoned or held indifferently will vanish without realization.

Pages:360

Self Help   **ISBN: *1-59462-644-8***   *MSRP $25.45* www.**bookjungle**.com *email: sales@bookjungle.com fax: 630-214-0564 mail: Book Jungle PO Box 2226 Champaign, IL 61825*

QTY

☐	**The Rosicrucian Cosmo-Conception Mystic Christianity** by *Max Heindel*	ISBN: *1-59462-188-8*	**$38.95**
	The Rosicrucian Cosmo-conception is not dogmatic, neither does it appeal to any other authority than the reason of the student. It is: not controversial, but is: sent forth in the, hope that it may help to clear...		*New Age Religion Pages 646*
☐	**Abandonment To Divine Providence** by *Jean-Pierre de Caussade*	ISBN: *1-59462-228-0*	**$25.95**
	"The Rev. Jean Pierre de Caussade was one of the most remarkable spiritual writers of the Society of Jesus in France in the 18th Century. His death took place at Toulouse in 1751. His works have gone through many editions and have been republished...		*Inspirational Religion Pages 400*
☐	**Mental Chemistry** by *Charles Haanel*	ISBN: *1-59462-192-6*	**$23.95**
	Mental Chemistry allows the change of material conditions by combining and appropriately utilizing the power of the mind. Much like applied chemistry creates something new and unique out of careful combinations of chemicals the mastery of mental chemistry...		*New Age Pages 354*
☐	**The Letters of Robert Browning and Elizabeth Barret Barrett 1845-1846 vol II**	ISBN: *1-59462-193-4*	**$35.95**
	by *Robert Browning* and *Elizabeth Barrett*		*Biographies Pages 596*
☐	**Gleanings In Genesis (volume I)** by *Arthur W. Pink*	ISBN: *1-59462-130-6*	**$27.45**
	Appropriately has Genesis been termed "the seed plot of the Bible" for in it we have, in germ form, almost all of the great doctrines which are afterwards fully developed in the books of Scripture which follow...		*Religion Inspirational Pages 420*
☐	**The Master Key** by *L. W. de Laurence*	ISBN: *1-59462-001-6*	**$30.95**
	In no branch of human knowledge has there been a more lively increase of the spirit of research during the past few years than in the study of Psychology, Concentration and Mental Discipline. The requests for authentic lessons in Thought Control, Mental Discipline and...		*New Age Business Pages 422*
☐	**The Lesser Key Of Solomon Goetia** by *L. W. de Laurence*	ISBN: *1-59462-092-X*	**$9.95**
	This translation of the first book of the "Lernegton" is now for the first time made accessible to students of Talismanic Magic was done, after careful collation and edition, from numerous Ancient Manuscripts in Hebrew, Latin, and French...		*New Age Occult Pages 92*
☐	**Rubaiyat Of Omar Khayyam** by *Edward Fitzgerald*	ISBN: *1-59462-332-5*	**$13.95**
	Edward Fitzgerald, whom the world has already learned, in spite of his own efforts to remain within the shadow of anonymity, to look upon as one of the rarest poets of the century, was born at Bredfield, in Suffolk, on the 31st of March, 1809. He was the third son of John Purcell...		*Music Pages 172*
☐	**Ancient Law** by *Henry Maine*	ISBN: *1-59462-128-4*	**$29.95**
	The chief object of the following pages is to indicate some of the earliest ideas of mankind, as they are reflected in Ancient Law, and to point out the relation of those ideas to modern thought.		*Religion History Pages 452*
☐	**Far-Away Stories** by *William J. Locke*	ISBN: *1-59462-129-2*	**$19.45**
	"Good wine needs no bush, but a collection of mixed vintages does. And this book is just such a collection. Some of the stories I do not want to remain buried for ever in the museum files of dead magazine-numbers an author's not unpardonable vanity..."		*Fiction Pages 272*
☐	**Life of David Crockett** by *David Crockett*	ISBN: *1-59462-250-7*	**$27.45**
	"Colonel David Crockett was one of the most remarkable men of the times in which he lived. Born in humble life, but gifted with a strong will, an indomitable courage, and unremitting perseverance...		*Biographies New Age Pages 424*
☐	**Lip-Reading** by *Edward Nitchie*	ISBN: *1-59462-206-X*	**$25.95**
	Edward B. Nitchie, founder of the New York School for the Hard of Hearing, now the Nitchie School of Lip-Reading, Inc, wrote "LIP-READING Principles and Practice". The development and perfecting of this meritorious work on lip-reading was an undertaking...		*How-to Pages 400*
☐	**A Handbook of Suggestive Therapeutics, Applied Hypnotism, Psychic Science**	ISBN: *1-59462-214-0*	**$24.95**
	by *Henry Munro*		*Health New Age Health/Self-help Pages 376*
☐	**A Doll's House: and Two Other Plays** by *Henrik Ibsen*	ISBN: *1-59462-112-8*	**$19.95**
	Henrik Ibsen created this classic when in revolutionary 1848 Rome. Introducing some striking concepts in playwriting for the realist genre, this play has been studied the world over.		*Fiction Classics Plays 308*
☐	**The Light of Asia** by *sir Edwin Arnold*	ISBN: *1-59462-204-3*	**$13.95**
	In this poetic masterpiece, Edwin Arnold describes the life and teachings of Buddha. The man who was to become known as Buddha to the world was born as Prince Gautama of India but he rejected the worldly riches and abandoned the reigns of power when...		*Religion History Biographies Pages 170*
☐	**The Complete Works of Guy de Maupassant** by *Guy de Maupassant*	ISBN: *1-59462-157-8*	**$16.95**
	"For days and days, nights and nights, I had dreamed of that first kiss which was to consecrate our engagement, and I knew not on what spot I should put my lips..."		*Fiction Classics Pages 240*
☐	**The Art of Cross-Examination** by *Francis L. Wellman*	ISBN: *1-59462-309-0*	**$26.95**
	Written by a renowned trial lawyer, Wellman imparts his experience and uses case studies to explain how to use psychology to extract desired information through questioning.		*How-to Science Reference Pages 408*
☐	**Answered or Unanswered?** by *Louisa Vaughan*	ISBN: *1-59462-248-5*	**$10.95**
	Miracles of Faith in China		*Religion Pages 112*
☐	**The Edinburgh Lectures on Mental Science (1909)** by *Thomas*	ISBN: *1-59462-008-3*	**$11.95**
	This book contains the substance of a course of lectures recently given by the writer in the Queen Street Hall, Edinburgh. Its purpose is to indicate the Natural Principles governing the relation between Mental Action and Material Conditions...		*New Age Psychology Pages 148*
☐	**Ayesha** by *H. Rider Haggard*	ISBN: *1-59462-301-5*	**$24.95**
	Verily and indeed it is the unexpected that happens! Probably if there was one person upon the earth from whom the Editor of this, and of a certain previous history, did not expect to hear again...		*Classics Pages 380*
☐	**Ayala's Angel** by *Anthony Trollope*	ISBN: *1-59462-352-X*	**$29.95**
	The two girls were both pretty; but Lucy who was twenty-one who supposed to be simple and comparatively unattractive, whereas Ayala was credited, as her Bombwhat romantic name might show, with poetic charm and a taste for romance. Ayala when her father died was nineteen...		*Fiction Pages 484*
☐	**The American Commonwealth** by *James Bryce*	ISBN: *1-59462-286-8*	**$34.45**
	An interpretation of American democratic political theory. It examines political mechanics and society from the perspective of Scotsman James Bryce		*Politics Pages 572*
☐	**Stories of the Pilgrims** by *Margaret P. Pumphrey*	ISBN: *1-59462-116-0*	**$17.95**
	This book explores pilgrims religious oppression in England as well as their escape to Holland and eventual crossing to America on the Mayflower, and their early days in New England...		*History Pages 268*

QTY

The Fasting Cure *by Sinclair Upton*   ISBN: *1-59462-222-1*   **$13.95**
In the Cosmopolitan Magazine for May, 1910, and in the Contemporary Review (London) for April, 1910, I published an article dealing with my experi-
ences in fasting. I have written a great many magazine articles, but never one which attracted so much attention...   New Age/Self Help/Health Pages 164

Hebrew Astrology *by Sepharial*   ISBN: *1-59462-308-2*   **$13.45**
In these days of advanced thinking it is a matter of common observation that we have left many of the old landmarks behind and that we are now pressing
forward to greater heights and to a wider horizon than that which represented the mind-content of our progenitors...   Astrology Pages 144

Thought Vibration or The Law of Attraction in the Thought World   ISBN: *1-59462-127-6*   **$12.95**
by William Walker Atkinson   Psychology/Religion Pages 144

Optimism *by Helen Keller*   ISBN: *1-59462-108-X*   **$15.95**
Helen Keller was blind, deaf, and mute since 19 months old, yet famously learned how to overcome these handicaps, communicate with the world, and
spread her lectures promoting optimism. An inspiring read for everyone...   Biographies Inspirational Pages 84

Sara Crewe *by Frances Burnett*   ISBN: *1-59462-360-0*   **$9.45**
In the first place, Miss Minchin lived in London. Her home was a large, dull, tall one, in a large, dull square, where all the houses were alike, and all the
sparrows were alike, and where all the door-knockers made the same heavy sound...   Childrens Classic Pages 88

The Autobiography of Benjamin Franklin *by Benjamin Franklin*   ISBN: *1-59462-135-7*   **$24.95**
The Autobiography of Benjamin Franklin has probably been more extensively read than any other American historical work, and no other book of its kind
has had such ups and downs of fortune. Franklin lived for many years in England, where he was agent...   Biographies History Pages 332

Name	
Email	
Telephone	
Address	
City, State ZIP	

☐ **Credit Card**   ☐ **Check / Money Order**

Credit Card Number	
Expiration Date	
Signature	

Please Mail to: Book Jungle
PO Box 2226
Champaign, IL 61825
or Fax to: 630-214-0564

ORDERING INFORMATION

web: *www.bookjungle.com*
email: *sales@bookjungle.com*
fax: *630-214-0564*
mail: *Book Jungle PO Box 2226 Champaign, IL 61825*
or PayPal *to sales@bookjungle.com*

Please contact us for bulk discounts

DIRECT-ORDER TERMS

**20% Discount if You Order
Two or More Books**
Free Domestic Shipping!
Accepted: Master Card, Visa,
Discover, American Express

Lightning Source UK Ltd.
Milton Keynes UK
UKOW021956120613

212174UK00011B/564/P